THE CASE OF THE
PURPLE UNICORN

THE CASE OF THE PURPLE UNICORN

A CONNER BRIGHT MYSTERY

ROBERT J. MCCARTER

LITTLE HUMMINGBIRD PUBLISHING

The Case of the Purple Unicorn

A Conner Bright Mystery

Version 1.0, January 2021

ISBN: 978-1-941153-54-3

Visit Robert's website at: RobertJMcCarter.com

Published by:

Little Hummingbird Publishing

P.O. Box 23518

Flagstaff, AZ 86002

www.LittleHummingbird.com

Little Hummingbird Publishing is a division of Arapas, Inc. Find more about Arapas at: www.Arapas.com.

CONNER BRIGHT MYSTERIES

Each Conner Bright Mystery is stand-alone, but things do change for Conner. This is the chronological order of the stories are:

- **The Case of the Purple Unicorn**
- **Chupacabra** (coming in 2021)
- *More coming soon!*

FOREWORD

This story, under a slightly different title, "Conner Bright and the Case of the Purple Unicorn" is available with a bunch of other stories of mine in two collections (just in case you'd like a bunch of stories to read):

- Creatures Featured: Thirteen Stories of Monsters and other Creatures
- Anomalous Readings: Thirteen Curious and Confounding Tales

CONNER BRIGHT AND THE CASE OF THE PURPLE UNICORN

The ringing of the phone is like a dentist's drill to my sodden consciousness. I groan, realizing I hadn't managed to get undressed when I tumbled into bed. Again. I feel for my cell phone on the nightstand, my hand connecting with a half-eaten microwave burrito before finding it.

"G'day, you got Bright," I say, remembering even in my hungover state to use my B-movie quality Australian accent.

"Got a job for you, but you've got to get here quick." The voice is feminine and a tad husky. Detective Trisha Sanchez. Why the hell is she calling me? After that jacked-up stakeout, I'm her least favorite private investigator in the Phoenix metro area.

"What kind of a job?" I say, my voice rough from too long in a noisy bar working as a bouncer and too many cheap beers afterward. I look around my shit hole of a bedroom. Dirty laundry, trash, the spring heat of the desert morning flowing in the open window. "And can they pay?"

An Australian accent is easy. Just elongate your vowels —"paay" instead of "pay"—and throw in the occasional "mate" and "g'day." In the desert southwest, that and changing my name to Conner Bright keeps my past at bay.

"They can. It's a murder, Bright, so get your ass out here now. No booze or I'll throw you in the drunk tank."

"Aces. Happy to help."

"Texting you the address now." She hangs up.

After some mouthwash for breakfast, I stop by the old cookie tin that sits on the top of my little entertainment center. It's got a shameful layer of dust on top and holds the ashes of my father inside. "Hey, Dad," I say, without a trace of an Australian accent. "I've got a case. An important one."

Sitting next to the tin is a DVD of *Crocodile Dundee*. My dad took me to that movie in 1986 when it came out. I was thirteen and loved it, but not as much as he did. When we exited, he'd said, "Now that's a man, son. That's a man."

I get out of my 1976 El Camino, my cowboy boots crunching on the dry ground as I approach the murder scene. It's a hot day, and since the El Camino doesn't have air-conditioning, I'm already sweating. I'm at a little ranch in the desert between Phoenix and Wickenburg, Arizona. This is a big deal. There's lots of cowboys and lots of guns around here, but not that many murders in the sticks.

I get the usual assortment of looks as I duck under the yellow tape. Looks of surprise from folks that don't know me, looks of recognition or disdain from those that do. The disdain belongs to Trisha Sanchez, the detective who called me in.

And the looks from the others, it's what I expect. I'm tall and slim; at 6'5" and 170 pounds, some people call me scarecrow. I've got a bowie knife with an eleven-inch blade on my belt, a crocodile claw hanging around my neck, and a wide-brimmed bush hat on my head, all to go with my Australian accent.

"G'day, Detective," I say, tipping my hat to Sanchez as she strides away from the murder scene. She's in her late thirties, short and wiry, wearing reflective sunglasses.

"Your client's in the house," she says, grabbing my arm and pulling me away. I resist a moment, watching Helen Montana, one of the medical examiners, leaning over the prone form of a gray-haired Mexican man that has a ragged hole in his chest.

"Where we goin'?" I ask.

"To see your client, Irene. She asked for someone to help her solve this murder."

"And you called me?" Something isn't right.

She pauses, her hand still locked around my bicep, her head jabbing back to the scene. "At this point we're ruling it an accident. The victim, Edwardo Campos, has got a big hole in his chest, and we found a bull running loose with blood on his horn."

She starts to pull me forward again toward the one-story ranch house. It's small with blue vinyl siding that was popular in the seventies. The blue has started to fade, and the house looks like it has seen better days.

"Then what the hell am I doin' here?"

Sanchez smiles, showing her perfectly white teeth, looking something like a shark. "The kid says she saw it happen."

I shrug.

"She says it was a man riding a purple unicorn that killed her great-uncle."

I almost don't go in. I almost march back to my El Camino until Sanchez says the magic words. "She's got cash." I think of the delinquent notices stacked on my little kitchen table. I think how I'd love not to buy the cheapest damn beer in the store.

It's surprisingly neat inside the house. Not fancy, but everything's put away, the wood floors swept, the old throw rugs shook out. The living room isn't much—an old couch with a brown blanket thrown over it, a wooden rocking chair, and a shelf full of books. No TV, no stereo. It looks very much like what this house probably looked like a hundred years ago.

Sitting awkwardly in the rocking chair is a tall deputy with blond hair. He gives Sanchez a brief look of relief before scurrying out.

And then I see the girl. She's got long black hair, big brown eyes, and is maybe eight years old. I almost leave again.

"Irene," Sanchez says, "this is Conner Bright. He's the private detective I was telling you about. He's got a reputation for dealing with unusual cases."

With that Sanchez leaves. I stand there awkwardly, my hands shoved into my jeans, wishing I hadn't answered the phone this morning.

The girl's wearing a purple shirt and has a stuffed unicorn on the couch next to her. On the table in front of her is a battered hardcover of *The Last Unicorn*.

Great. Of course she saw a purple unicorn. She's obsessed with them.

"Where are you parents?" I ask.

She just shakes her head. Ah hell, she's an orphan too.

I lower myself into the rocking chair, wishing the hard seat was padded. The room smells of must and wood polish. "You got any family?"

She shakes her head again, her hands sitting placidly in her lap.

"I'm sorry about what happened to your great-uncle out there."

Her brow furrows and she stares at me a moment before saying, "Where you from?" Judging from her uncle and her appearance, I expect her to have a Mexican accent, but she doesn't. Not a trace.

"Australia," I lie. But it's a lie I tell everyone. "A little place called Scatterwood deep in the outback."

"You don't believe I saw a unicorn." She says it straight up, her voice steady, her eyes clear.

I shake my head.

"I did," she says, her voice too hard for someone so young. "And you have to prove it." She pulls out a wad of hundred-dollar bills from her pocket and slaps them on the coffee table in front of her. I notice light red stains on her hands and I imagine them pressed against her dead great-uncle's chest.

I know I should say no, but three thousand is a lot for me. A whole lot. I rub my suddenly sweating palms on my jeans. I'm dying for a drink. That would clear my head. Help me think this through.

"Well?" she asks.

I get up and start pacing. "Why don't you tell me what you saw."

The girl talks, I pace, my feet finding squeaky boards in the old floor. The money is in a jumbled pile on the coffee table in front of her. I want it even more than I want a drink.

"Been here for a few months," she says. "Came after the accident . . ." Her face darkens, and she blinks several times. "We moved around a lot, Mama, Papa, and me. We picked grapes in California, pecans in Oregon."

"Your parents were illegals?" I ask.

She nods. "But I was born here. After the accident, Uncle

Ed came and got me. He was afraid they'd send me back to Mexico."

"Tell me about your great-uncle," I say.

She shrugs. "He raises cows, rides horses."

I look at the wad of hundred-dollar bills and then back to her, doubting that was all he did.

"And last night?"

Irene pauses, her hands finally leaving her lap as she wraps them around her chest and shivers. "Uncle Ed was so happy. Said things would be changing today, like a birthday party but better. Said it would be good. We were reading when the animals started making noise. He took his gun and told me to stay.

"I wasn't scared until I heard a shout. I went to the window and peeked through the curtain. That's when I saw it."

"The unicorn?" I ask, keeping my tone as even as possible.

She nods. "The moon was full so I could see good. At first I thought it was a horse with a man riding it. But then I saw the horn and the dark purple fur. Uncle Ed was real surprised. That man spurred the unicorn hard, and it ran down my uncle, its horn hitting him... right in the... He... I..." She trails off into soft sobs. I feel for the kid. She's suffered way too many losses in the past few months.

The tears don't last long. She takes a deep breath, holds it for a few beats, and slowly lets it out. She wipes the tears from her cheeks, her eyes hardening. "The man got off the unicorn and came in here."

"What did you do?"

"I hid behind the door. He walked in like he had been here before. Went right to the kitchen. I hid behind the couch and watched. I couldn't see much. There was banging, crashing, and a bunch of beeps. He marched out holding some papers."

"Did he see you? Did you get a good look at him?"

She shakes her head. "He had a bandana over his mouth. I don't think he saw me. He walked right out, got on his unicorn, and rode away."

I nod and walk into the small kitchen. One of the plain handmade wooden cabinets is open, cans spilling out onto the counter and the floor. In the cabinet is a small metal safe embedded into the wall. The door is ajar, and the safe is empty.

"Is that where you got the money?" I ask after I walk back into the living room.

Irene nods, her hands back onto her lap, her eyes way too calm.

It's a hot day and the corpse of Edwardo Campos is going to stink to high heaven soon. The smell of blood and urine and horse manure is already overpowering.

"It looks like a horn did this," Helen Montana says, pulling away the bloodied cowboy shirt that used to be a powder blue. There's been a lot of foot traffic, but I did find a few fresh hoof-prints leading to the corpse. She gets up, brushing absently at her ponytailed blonde hair. Helen is a tall, big-boned woman with blue eyes and a great smile. She's my age at around forty. There's been sparks, and we've briefly dated a few times, but never a sustained flame. Working with her is always a bit awkward.

She walks several paces back to a yellow CSI marker where I located the hoofprints right next to a shotgun. "It looks like he was hit here and thrown back."

"The bull did it?" I ask.

"I'll know more when I do the autopsy."

I nod, glancing back to the faded blue ranch house.

"Sorry, Conner," she says, and I hear that sweetness in her voice that makes work hard.

"Did they get a blood sample from the bull's horn?" I ask.

She chuckles and looks over to a corral where two deputies are trying to get a rope around the bull. He's a big Hereford and doesn't appear to be cooperating. "Maybe you should go show them how it's done."

I shake my head, feeling uncomfortable. Helen was born in upstate New York and has a thing for cowboys. Could explain her interest in a mess like me.

Sanchez walks up, her arms folded. "You taking the case?"

"Any other witnesses?" I ask, pointing at a smaller building back behind the blue house.

Sanchez shakes her head. "Campos used to have a ranch hand living there. The neighbors told us he left a few months ago before the girl got here. Said they were close, that the old man treated him like a son, but something happened."

"Did you call CPS, Child Protective Services?"

She nods. "Doesn't look like they can get out here today."

"Why the hell not?"

"Budget cuts. Short staffed. You know the drill."

"And what about Irene?"

Sanchez chuckles and smiles at me again. "You take the case, you take the girl." She walks away looking like she's having the time of her life, paying me back for that stakeout with this mess.

I go help the deputies with the bull. Not that I want to get into the corral with a ton of pissed off beef. I need to think. And to think, I need to move. Everyone, including Detective Sanchez, knows I need the cash. But taking a little girl's money on a wild-goose chase doesn't seem proper.

I climb over the fence and hop down onto the churned brown dirt of the corral. It stinks of horse and cow, but at least it doesn't smell of death. The jolt of the hop doesn't do my sacrum any good, and I feel each and every one of my old rodeo injuries. I rode bulls for a while, but mostly worked as a rodeo clown—keeping other riders safe was the right kind of crazy for me.

"You're just makin' the old boy mad," I shout to the two deputies. One is the lanky blond from the house. "Back away." They comply promptly.

I scrape some oats out of the bottom of the feed trough and get the specimen collection swab from the tall deputy and amble over toward the bull.

Those deputies may have been born and raised in Arizona, but they ain't no cowboys. They were afraid and trying to overpower an animal that's five times their weight. Stupid.

"Hi ya, boy," I say gently as I approach, the hand with the oats outstretched. I keep my eye on the bull and walk slowly. This is no rodeo bull used to bucking guys like me off. This fellow's older, probably kept around for stud duties. He didn't want to fight, but he didn't want to be bullied either.

People think cows are dumb, but they ain't. They seek safety and comfort just like the rest of us. The bull's big brown eyes finally leave mine and flick to the handful of oats. I'm two paces away and I stop walking, the final choice has to be his.

My left hand has the swab in it, and I hold it just back from the oats. I'd be a fool to spring it on him while he was eating. His nostrils flair and his eyes flick to the swab and back to the oats. He doesn't like the sharp alcohol scent of the swab, but he wants the oats.

I stand there like I don't care and just keep talking to him. He eventually takes two steps forward, his soft mouth in my hand as his rough tongue licks up the oats. I wipe the swab against the red stain on his horn, and when he's done eating, I back slowly away.

A crowd has gathered, and there's a smattering of applause.

When I'm clear of the bull, I look back and see Helen holding Irene on the other side of the corral. Detective Sanchez is there, a question on her face.

"The girl is traumatized," I say to Sanchez. We're out of earshot of Helen and Irene, who are both staring at us as we walk the dirt driveway. "She needs a professional."

"The system sucks," she says, "but the girl needs something to do, and running around with you trying to find a purple unicorn might be better than her hanging out in the sheriff's office."

I'm about to say something stupid when it occurs to me that this must be Sanchez's way of looking out for the girl. But why me? "What about the robbery? There's somethin' that ain't right."

She shrugs and points towards the bull. "I've got the killer right there. As to the money, the old man just realized he bought a bunch of Home Depot stock on a whim back in the eighties. He's suddenly rich, that explains the money, and besides, the safe wasn't forced open. Until I have evidence to the contrary, I'm done."

I nod and look back at the girl. Helen has her by the hand and is walking her away from the crime scene and towards the pasture. The girl needs someone, that much is certain. But me? A mostly drunk, past-his-prime cowboy pretending to be Australian?

"Look, Bright," Sanchez says. "Just take the girl for the day. Take any clue you can find and run it down with her. I'll call you when the social workers are ready for her."

Sanchez walks away and starts barking orders. I don't fight it. I owe her.

I keep Irene in the house while Helen finishes with the corpse and hauls him away.

It's odd that the murderer wanted those papers, but didn't care about the money. And that damn unicorn keeps tripping me up. Maybe there was no robbery. Maybe Irene knew the combination and got into the safe herself.

I'm standing in the mess of a kitchen staring off into space when I notice Irene looking at me. Her eyes have that too-wide look of shock. That's why she's been so restrained. The poor kid is in shock. Sanchez was right, she needs something to do.

"All righty then," I say, stooping down and picking up a can. "Get over here and help me clean this up."

"Clean?" Irene says.

I nod. "There could be a clue here, so we're gonna clean up this mess and see what we can find."

While Irene is in the kitchen, I go searching Edwardo's bedroom. It's small and neat, with a twin bed, an old wooden chest at the end, a small closet, and a cross on the wall.

I start in the closet, going through the pale blue cowboy shirts—the man liked to dress the same every day—and patting down the two dark blue blazers. Each of them has a matchbook from the same place. The Sugar and Spice, a "gentlemen's club" in downtown Phoenix.

So the old man liked to look at young women.

"Did your Uncle Ed go out much?" I ask Irene back in the kitchen.

Irene nods. "Every Saturday night. He didn't think I knew,

but he snuck out after I went to bed. Stayed out real late. He always came back smelling like smoke." She wrinkles her nose.

It's Monday morning, Edwardo was killed Sunday night. Maybe something happened at Sugar and Spice. I show Irene the matchbooks.

"What is it?" she asks.

"A clue, Irene. It's a clue."

The Sugar and Spice is a pinkish building with bright neon that sits between a bank and a fast-food joint off a busy street in central Phoenix. I shift uncomfortably in the seat of the El Camino as I drive by for the fourth time. It's Irene sitting next to me that makes me feel uncomfortable.

The fifth time I drive by, Irene sighs and says, "Just pull in."

I park behind the building.

"Are we going in?" Irene asks.

"You're kiddin', right?"

"I know what goes on in there. Men look at girls." She ends by rolling her eyes.

My reputation's bad enough without dragging an eight-year-old into a strip club right before turning her over to CPS. "Not gonna happen, love," I say as I get out the car. I walk over and open the door for her. She looks puzzled, but gets out and follows me to the McDonald's next door. As I do this, I'm convinced that I'm not the only man that's dropped off a little girl at this McDonald's before ducking into Sugar and Spice.

She doesn't complain, but she grabs my hand and holds it as we cross the hot asphalt. Her hand feels so small in mine, and I look down at her and she's looking at me with a tiny smile on her face. That look of trust scares the hell out of me.

The inside of Sugar and Spice smells of desperation, with a bored blond dancing and a few rumpled men watching. I give the bartender a twenty and show him the picture of Edwardo Campos that Irene gave me. He tells me Edwardo was there the night before last, buying drinks and celebrating like he'd just won the lottery or something.

On the way out of Sugar and Spice, I'm confused. I have no motive for murder, and no idea why a robber would leave behind a wad of cash—or ride a purple unicorn, for that matter.

I'm not looking and collide with a man on his way in while I'm on the way out, the Phoenix heat swirling around us.

"Sorry, mate," I say, looking at the stranger. He's got on alligator-skin cowboy boots, a Stetson hat, sharp green eyes, and a sneer. He's almost as tall as me, but a lot beefier.

"Watch it, buddy," he grumbles, moving past quickly. I'm distracted by his boots, which would make a fine addition to my Australian cowboy look.

I get halfway to the El Camino when Irene runs up and wraps her arms around me. "That's him," she whispers between gulping breaths. "The man that came into my house. That killed Uncle Ed."

"How do you know?"

"The boots. The eyes. I'll never forget them."

An El Camino is a crappy car to tail someone in. Especially mine. With its shiny blue paint job and tricked-out rims, it stands out. This car is the one thing in my life that I truly take care of. I love it. It's a car, but it's got a bed like a truck. It's rare. It used to be my dad's.

Irene is sitting right next to me, eyes wide. She smells of cheap beef, french fries, and fear. Her closeness feels strangely good.

We follow Alligator Boots in his red Ford F-150 from Sugar and Spice to a Circle K where he stops for gas. I pull into the carpet place next door. When he ducks into the Circle K, I make to get out of the car, but Irene grabs me.

"Don't go," she says. "Please."

I get lost in those big brown eyes of hers. I'm not used to someone needing me.

"I'll be right back. No worries." Those eyes don't look like they believe me.

I walk casually over to the truck and place my cell phone in the back. What I see there makes me gasp. It's a long horn with spiral ridges running its length. It's an honest-to-god unicorn horn. I'm dizzy for a moment. Did Irene really see what she thought she saw?

As I look closer, I see that the tip of the horn is rough, as if it broke off, and the other end has an odd leather harness on it.

I rush back to the car, my heart pounding hard.

––––––––––––

It feels strange, like I'm missing something. I've left Irene with the morgue's receptionist. I had called in on a burner phone I bought at the Circle K to have Sanchez trace my cell so I could keep tabs on Alligator Boots. She told me Helen needed to see me and it was urgent.

Helen is pacing when I walk in. Her blue eyes are a bit wide and remind me of Irene's. Does Helen need me too?

The corpse of Edwardo Campos is laid out on a metal table, the wound to his chest all that much more shocking being exposed—no shirt to hide it, no blood to mask it. It's a big, red hole near his heart.

The morgue is pretty small. A couple of shining tables for the dead with bright lights mounted above. A wall of drawers for bodies to be stored in. Except for the ragged wound in Edwardo's chest, the place is spotless and smells strongly of antiseptic.

Helen's biting her lip and stands me next to the body, showing me a stainless-steel tray. In it is what looks like a piece of bone about the size of an almond. Like a piece of rib or something.

"So?" I ask, shrugging my shoulders.

"The blood you got from the bull's horn is his. But . . . I pulled *this* out of him," she says, like she's telling me the Pope is secretly a woman or something.

I give her a blank stare. I'm clueless.

She drags me over to a big, round magnifying glass and holds the tray underneath it, giving me a pointed look. I lean close and look at the little piece of bone. It's pointed and has a distinct spiral ridge. When I look back at Helen, I'm smiling. She looks worried.

"That ain't no cow horn," I say.

She shakes her head.

"Good on ya, Helen," I say, kissing her on the cheek. "You just made my case."

"What? Conner, unicorns don't exist. How can this be?"

I shrug. "Don't know. What I do know is I just saw the mate to that piece in the back of an F-150."

We're back in the El Camino heading out of Phoenix towards my place. I'm tired and hungry and don't know what else to do.

Sanchez won't go after Alligator Boots. Won't tell officers to look for an F-150 with a unicorn horn in the back, says she'd be risking her reputation and won't do that for me. She wants more evidence.

Irene's smile is a mile wide. She looks so much more like a kid now. She's happy because I told her what Helen found and what I saw in the back of that F-150. Told her that I believe her. Her smile warms my wilted old heart.

It's near rush hour and the Phoenix traffic is thick as ants on honey. We're moving slowly forward in the stifling heat.

Phoenix is a flat and boring expanse except for the occasional outcrop of craggy stone. The city streets are a monotony of urban sprawl with strip malls, cookie-cutter houses, and the ubiquitous Circle Ks.

"So do you think it was a real unicorn?" Irene asks, her voice all bubbly and light.

I shrug my shoulders. Given the harness that was on the horn, I doubt that. I didn't get to telling her that part, and with her lit up like this, I just can't.

In the rearview, I catch a flash of a bright red truck weaving its way through traffic. My face falls.

"What's wrong, Conner?" Irene asks.

"Nothin', love," I lie. I point at the glove compartment. "There's a bottle of water in there. You best drink in this heat."

She nods and dutifully pulls out the water bottle and takes a drink. My eyes keep flicking to the rearview mirror looking for that red truck. Maybe it's Mr. Alligator Boots. Maybe he got wise to me following him.

At a stoplight, I pull out the burner phone and text Sanchez, *Check location of both phones.*

A minute later, as the traffic is finally starting to ease up, she texts back. *Same location.*

We didn't have the tail long. I saw him briefly right behind me and then he was gone, talking a left and speeding off.

When we're past the city and closer to my house, we pull into yet another Circle K, my stomach grumbling and my head pounding. I needed food and a drink. A stiff drink. I take Irene in. She holds my hand the whole time while I pick up a few microwave burritos and some cookies for us, and she picks out some potato chips.

I stop in front of the refrigerated section. I have to let go of Irene's hand to open the door. My hand's shaking a bit, my body screaming for alcohol. And there it is. Row after row of beer, an obscene number of choices. Dark beer, light beer, fancy beer, cheap beer, foreign beer.

Beer reminds me of Tommy Wilkins. Of the sickening sound of his scream when I ran him over. You'd think it would make me drink less, but it's done just the opposite.

I was sixteen and at a high school party near Globe, Arizona, where I grew up. Tommy and I fought over a girl whose name I can't even remember. We were both drunk, and I was trying to leave and he wouldn't get out of the way, banging on the hood of my old Toyota pickup and screaming at me while I revved the engine. My foot slipped off the clutch and . . .

It was big news in Arizona. I did my time in the juvenile system, had my records sealed, but people around here remember my name. That's why I changed it, even though it broke my dad's heart. That's the reason behind the whole fake Australian thing. That's why my life is such a—

"What?" I ask. Irene had just said something.

She smiles and points at the vitamin water. "Can I have one of those? The purple one, please."

I blink at her a few times and nod, grabbing two of the plastic bottles and handing them to her. I turn my back on the obscene array of alcohol. Maybe tonight I can sleep without the beer.

I'm not thinking well. I drive right to my ten acres, a few miles from the Circle K, and pull in. Irene is babbling on like happy kids do, her words bright shards bouncing around my car. My fatigue and her happiness seem to lull me into a peaceful state. She goes on and on that when she grows up she's going to make a "My Little Unicorn" toy for girls, like the one already made for horses. That since unicorns are real, and once she finds one and gets her picture taken with it, everyone girl in the world will want one.

I still haven't told her about the harness.

"Maybe instead of 'My Little Unicorn,'" she says as I unlock the door to my dingy single-wide trailer, "I will name it after you." She's beaming at me now, like I'm someone important. "I'll call it 'Unicorn Bright.' That's a wonderful name."

I step into the house and am nodding when the clenched fist of Alligator Boots connects with my jaw, fiery pain radiating through the left side of my face. He was waiting behind the door.

As I go down, I curse my fatigue. He had tailed me long enough to get a look at my license plate. From there it wasn't hard to get my address or break in.

Irene screams and our food goes tumbling to the floor. On my way down I get a look at the chaotic mess of my living room. Dust covering the flat screen, piles of clothes, trash, dirty carpet.

I have a horrible realization: If I can't take care of my own living room, how am I going to take care of Irene? The thought doesn't last long. My head bounces off the carpet with a sharp crack and darkness descends.

I wake up with a start, the light of the full moon shining above me, hard ground below me, and cool air on my skin. My head is pounding and my jaw aches. My mouth is dry and my stomach clenches. I roll over and try to vomit, but there's nothing in me.

I hear the snort of a horse and bolt upright, the motion making my stomach try to empty itself again.

"Stand up," Alligator Boots says. He's mounted on what looks like a purple unicorn, a white horn jutting from its forehead, its coat a dark purple. In the moonlight it's hard to see the harness on the horse's head, but I know it's there.

"Why might I be doing that?" I ask, trying to hide the pain and desperation in my voice.

"Because if you don't, it will go badly for the girl."

We're back behind my trailer. It used to be a horse corral, back when I could afford to keep a horse. Now it's a falling down fence and a weedy expanse of dirt. Back behind the horse and Alligator Boots, I see the trailer, my El Camino, and his F-150 with a horse trailer attached.

"What?" I ask, trying desperately to get my mind to turn over.

Alligator Boots staged Edwardo Campos's death as an attack by a unicorn. Why? So Irene, a little girl obsessed with unicorns, would see it. Would talk about it. Would be dismissed. He put Edwardo's blood on that bull's horn. He also took something from the safe, just papers and not money.

This was all about Irene. The way her great-uncle had died had been a show for her.

Alligator Boots points to his right and I see Irene. She's tied to one of my cheap plastic chairs. She's gagged and her eyes are wide, her cheeks stained with tears.

I nod, make a show of getting up, and then slump back to the ground with a grunt. "What is it you needed from that safe?" I'm leaning on my right side, where my bowie knife should be, but he's taken it.

"Stand up!" he yells.

"You're the ranch hand Mr. Campos had a recent falling out with, ain't ya? The one that was once like a son to him."

He pulls a gun from his side and points it at Irene. "Stand. Now." He's not yelling anymore and that's a bad sign.

I slowly get into a squatting position. I feel in my right boot. That knife is still there.

I remember what Sanchez had told me about Edwardo Campos's recently remembered stock. What the bartender at Sugar and Spice had said when I showed him Edwardo's picture. How Edwardo had hinted to Irene that things were about to change for her.

"He wrote you out of his will," I say as I pull the knife from my boot and hold it behind my back, shakily standing up. "That's what ya took, the will that left everything to Irene. I'm guessing he hadn't signed it yet, but was about to. He had told all his buddies at Sugar and Spice about his windfall, about how he was leaving it all to his delightful niece that loves unicorns and the color purple. Someone there told ya."

Alligator Boots doesn't speak. He spurs the horse hard, and it leaps forward. As I stand there, I have empathy for Edwardo Campos. He came out in the middle of the night under the bright moonlight expecting a coyote and saw a galloping unicorn bearing down on him. He had the shotgun in his hand, but he didn't use it. His grandniece had been babbling about unicorns, and now seeing one made him dumb for an instant, just one small instant.

Adrenaline dumps into my bloodstream, my heart pounding in my ears in time with the thundering of the hooves. But I don't move. I stand there swaying, still trying to get my bearings, hoping my body still remembers my time at the rodeo.

I wonder what Detective Sanchez will do if she finds my body just like Edwardo's, if she has a hysterical girl that talks about yet another man being run through by a purple unicorn. Once, she might brush off, twice, never. It's all over for Alligator Boots, even if I don't survive. This thought gives me comfort. Briefly.

But what of Irene? I remember how she clung to me outside Sugar and Spice, how she sat so close to me in the El Camino, how she held my hand in the Circle K. It felt strange, but good, to be depended on. My eyes flick to her. I can't hear her over the pounding hooves or through her gag, but it's clear she's screaming.

The unicorn is upon me. I smell dust, paint, and its sweat. I quickly rotate my body around, moving just to the side. I pull the knife from behind my back. I do what I need to do.

I wake up slowly and groan, realizing I'm fully dressed again. I'm slumped in a half-seated position, my lower back and my neck aching, my mouth dry as the desert.

"Take it easy." I'm not sure who it is at first, a woman with a sweet voice. Helen.

And then the events of the last day tumble onto me like a monsoon cloudburst. I bolt upright and open my eyes. "Irene," I croak.

"She's fine," Helen says, putting a hand on my back, a gentle smile on her lips.

"Where is she?" Part of me feels silly. I hardly know the girl. Another part of me is desperate for her to be okay.

"CPS came while you were sleeping. She's just fine, Conner."

I nod and rub at my face, trying to wake myself up, feeling several days of stubble. I remember the charging unicorn. I remember rotating out of the way and jamming my knife through one of those alligator skin boots. I remember him screaming and falling off that spray-painted horse, struggling to get up. Me punching him in the face. Him lying still. Untying Irene. Her sobbing and clinging to me while I called Detective Sanchez.

"They took her," I mumble, mostly to myself.

Helen is looking at me, her soft blue eyes searching my face like I'm not the man she knows.

I remember what it had felt like as Irene clung to me while we waited for the sheriff's deputies to arrive. How the ambulance had come and I had refused it and Irene had refused to leave me. How they had hauled Alligator Boots away. How Helen had finally come and we had gone into the trailer. I had given Irene my bed and held her hand for hours until she fell asleep and then stumbled out to the couch. Helen had insisted on staying.

"That horn," Helen says, pulling out her phone and showing me a picture that looks like a whale with a unicorn horn sticking out of its head. "It was real. This is a narwhal, that tusk is some crazy tooth."

It all makes sense... except for how I feel.

I look up to the tin of ashes on top of my entertainment center. I lever myself up, stumble over, and say, "Hey, Dad. The girl's safe." I reach down, my head screaming at me, and pick up a stray piece of paper, a microwave burrito wrapper.

"What are you doing?" Helen asks.

"I'm cleaning up." She's staring at me, like she doesn't know me. Like we've never danced or touched or had meals together. "Will you help me?"

The door is a faded yellow and the neighborhood's somewhat

faded, too. It might have been cheery three decades ago, but now it's looking a little sad.

It's been ten days since I met Irene, and two days since I've had a drink. I would have come sooner, but I swore to myself I wouldn't do it unless I had been dry for at least two days. My hand is shaking as I knock.

A plump woman with a pinched face answers the door.

"I'm here to see Irene," I say. "I called earlier."

She nods, lets me in, and leaves me in the living room. There's a TV playing loudly with strange blue creatures on it dancing around. There's a couple of kids, much younger than Irene, watching it, their eyes wide.

And then she's there. This time I'm expecting it and kneel down before she gets to me. "You okay?" I whisper.

She hugs me hard. She nods and sniffs. I can feel her tears on my shoulder. I can feel my own tears on my cheek. "What took you so long?" She says it gently but it feels like a horse kicked me in the chest.

"I was . . . I . . ." I stammer. "I was trying to . . ." I can't finish. I can't tell this girl that I was trying to be worthy of her. That I have been ever since we met. That I will be as long as she'll have me.

I don't know if she understands, but she hugs me even harder and that's enough.

MORE MYSTERY?

If you want more Conner Bright, your best bet is to sign up for my newsletter at RobertJMcCarter.com/newsletter. You'll get some free ebooks and you'll find out when the next case is available. Or go to RobertJMcCarter.com/ConnerBright for a complete list of books.

If you want more mystery, I've got a two other series you might want to check out:

Carterville

Carterville, AZ

Population: 286. People with powers: 198

Just a sleepy former mining town turned tourist haven in the mountains of Northern Arizona until the "incident." The meteor that gave everyone in the town powers, but only while near Carterville.

There are two books out in the

series with another novel coming in 2021. Find out more at CartervilleAZ.com.

Walter Anchor, Ghost Detective

WALTER ANCHOR: HE'S A GHOST trying to solve his own murder. A ghost with plenty of unfinished business.

Emily: She died at the age of four and still looks it but she's been dead for eighty years. She has a nose for murder.

Together: They solve murders.

There are six cases so far. Be sure to check out the omnibus edition, *Unfinished Business,* which has all six cases in one volume. Find out more at RobertJMcCarter.com/WalterAnchor.

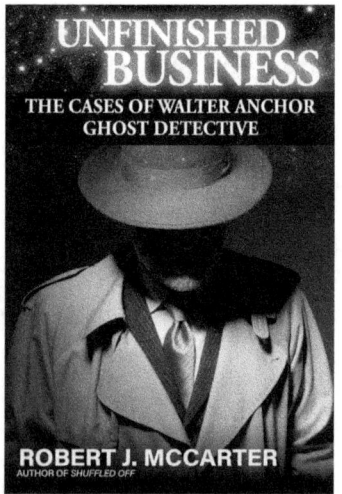

ABOUT THE AUTHOR

Robert J. McCarter is the author of over a dozen novels, nine novellas, and dozens of short stories. He is a finalist for the *Writers of the Future* contest and his stories have appeared or are forthcoming in *The Saturday Evening Post, Pulphouse Fiction Magazine, Fiction River, Andromeda Spaceways Inflight Magazine*, and numerous anthologies.

A recent effort is a serialized novel called *Woody and June Versus the Apocalypse*, a story of adventure and love and taking things (even the apocalypse) in stride. Of his novel, *Seeing Forever*, Kirkus Reviews says, "Sci-fi as it should be: engaging, moving, and grand in scope."

He lives in the mountains of Arizona with his amazing wife and his ridiculously adorable dogs.

Find out more at:
RobertJMcCarter.com

BOOKS BY ROBERT J. MCCARTER

Conner Bright Mysteries

- **The Case of the Purple Unicorn**
- **Chupacabra** (coming in 2021)
- *More coming soon!*

Carterville Mysteries

- **Out of a Christmas Sky**
- **Unnamed 2021 Novel**
- **The Blood of Carterville**

For a complete list go to CartervilleAZ.com

Walter Anchor, Ghost Detective Stories

- **Case 1: Detecting Haley** (also part of *Life After: Stories of Life, Death, and the Places in Between*)
- **Case 2: The Ghost Bride's Gift**
- **Case 3: A Long Hard Fall**
- **Case 4: Death of a Dentist**
- **Case 5: A Hollywood Kind of a Murder**
- **Case 6: The Red Arrow Murders**
- **Unfinished Business: The Cases of Walter**

Anchor Ghost Detective

For a complete list of Walter Anchor stories, go to RobertJMcCarter.com/WalterAnchor

Short Stores Collections

- Life After: Stories of Life, Death, and the Places in Between
- Anomalous Readings: Thirteen Curious and Confounding Tales
- Creatures Featured: Thirteen Stories of Monsters and other Creatures

Novels in the "Ghost's Memoir" world:

Find out more at ShuffledOff.com

The Woody and June versus the Apocalypse Series

Find out more at WoodyAndJune.com

The Neutrinoman and Lightningirl Series

Find out more at Neutrinoman.com

Other Novels:

- Seeing Forever
- Where the Past Belongs: An Angelica and Ash Time Travel Adventure

For a more information, go to RobertJMcCarter.com

THE CASE OF THE PURPLE UNICORN

Private investigator and Arizona native Conner Bright tries to hide from his past with a b-movie quality Australian accent, alligator skin boots, and a bowie knife strapped to his side, but it always seems to catch up to him.

When a little girl swears she saw her great uncle murdered by a purple unicorn, Conner takes the case expecting to face nothing more than a little girl's overactive imagination. But in this short story, Conner must confront his past and put his life on the line to protect his young client.

From Robert J. McCarter, the author of *Unfinished Business* comes a private investigator and a case like no others.

$5.99
Little Hummingbird Publishing
EBOOK EDITION AVAILABLE
RobertJMcCarter.com

ISBN 9781941153543

90000

9 781941 153543

SOFT SPOKEN WORDS

CHELSEA S. THOMAS